Happy

Robert Caisley

A Samuel French Acting Edition

FOUNDED 1830

SAMUELFRENCH.COM
SAMUELFRENCH-LONDON.CO.UK

FOR PRODUCTION ENQUIRIES

UNITED STATES AND CANADA
Info@SamuelFrench.com
1-866-598-8449

UNITED KINGDOM AND EUROPE
Theatre@SamuelFrench-London.co.uk
020-7255-4302

Each title is subject to availability from Samuel French, depending
upon country of performance. Please be aware that *HAPPY* may not be
licensed by Samuel French in your territory. Professional and amateur
producers should contact the nearest Samuel French office or licensing
partner to verify availability.

MUSIC USE NOTE

Licensees are solely responsible for obtaining formal written permission from copyright owners to use copyrighted music in the performance of this play and are strongly cautioned to do so. If no such permission is obtained by the licensee, then the licensee must use only original music that the licensee owns and controls. Licensees are solely responsible and liable for all music clearances and shall indemnify the copyright owners of the play(s) and their licensing agent, Samuel French, against any costs, expenses, losses and liabilities arising from the use of music by licensees. Please contact the appropriate music licensing authority in your territory for the rights to any incidental music.

IMPORTANT BILLING AND CREDIT REQUIREMENTS

If you have obtained performance rights to this title, please refer to your licensing agreement for important billing and credit requirements.

HAPPY was first produced in a rolling world premiere, as part of the National New Play Network's Continued Life Program at the following theatres:

HAPPY opened on October 19, 2012 at Montana Repertory Theatre (Gregory T. Johnson, Artistic Director) in Missoula, Montana. The director was Jere Hodgin; the set design was by Jason J. McDaniel, featuring original paintings and sculptures by Bradley Allen, Kevin Bell and Jennifer Combe; the costume design was by Laura H. Alvarez; the lighting and sound design was by Morgan Cerovski; the production dramaturg was Anna Dulba-Barnett; the stage manager was Randi Berg. The cast was as follows:

ALFRED	Andy Myers
EVA	Hillary Sea Bard
EDUARDO	Andrew Roa
MELINDA	Angela Billadeau

HAPPY opened on November 30, 2012 at New Theatre (Ricky J. Martinez, Artistic Director; Eileen Suarez, Managing Director) in Miami, Florida. The director was Ricky J. Martinez; the set design was by Ricky J. Martinez, featuring original visual art by Theresa Marie Callouri; the lighting design was by Eric J. Cantrell; the sound design was by R. Kent Wilson; the production stage manager was Jerry Jensen. The cast was as follows:

ALFRED	Scott Douglas Wilson
EVA	Maria Corina Ramirez
EDUARDO	Ernesto Miyares
MELINDA	Jessica Marion Welch

HAPPY opened on April 5, 2013 at 6th Street Playhouse (Craig A. Miller, Executive Artistic Director) in Santa Rosa, California. The director was Lennie Dean; the set design was by Jesse Dreikosen, featuring original sculptures by Boback Emad; the costume design was by Liz Fay Smith; the lighting design was by April George; the sound design was by Craig A. Miller; the production stage manager was Beulah Vega. The cast was as follows:

ALFRED	Edward McCloud
EVA	Rose Roberts
EDUARDO	Brian Glenn Bryson
MELINDA	Liz Jahren

HAPPY opened on May 30, 2013 at New Jersey Repertory Company (Gabor Barabas, Executive Producer; SuzAnne Barabas, Artistic Director; Jane E. Huber, Managing Director) in Long Branch, New Jersey. The director was SuzAnne Barabas; the scenic design was by Jessica Parks; the costume design was by Patricia E. Doherty; the lighting design was by Jill Nagle; the sound design was by Merek Royce Press; the stage manager was Jennifer Tardibuono. The cast was as follows:

ALFRED................................Michael Irvin Pollard
EVA ....Susan Maris
EDUARDO..................................Mark Light-Orr
MELINDA ....Wendy Peace

The author wishes to thank Jere Hodgin, Marta Praeger, Jason Loewith, Jojo Ruff and NNPN, the Missoula Writers Colony, Ricky J. Martinez, Eileen Suarez, Lori Celaya, the Idaho Commission on the Arts and National Endowment for the Arts for their support during the development of this play.

CHARACTERS

ALFRED REHM – 40s; he is happy

MELINDA – his wife; 40s; she is happy

EDUARDO – his friend; 60s; extraordinarily vibrant for his age; speaks with a slight accent; he is happy

EVA – 20s, she is not happy

SETTING

The entire action of the play takes place in Eduardo's apartment, an artist's loft cum living space. There are high ceilings, tall windows, and lots of light.

Whatever furniture exists, it exists amidst the artistic clutter. There are several "industrial" sculptures in progress. One is draped in a tarp.

The space is great; the neighborhood is not.

This play is dedicated to Jere Hodgin

Happiness is the perpetual possession of being well-deceived.

– Lytton Strachey

ONE

(In the darkness before the lights come up we hear a police siren and other sounds of the inner-city.)

(At rise: **ALFRED**, *with a bottle of wine and his briefcase, stands awkwardly just inside the entryway to the apartment, in a puddle of water.)*

(He is drenched from the waist down and is trying to dry himself off, unsuccessfully, with a handkerchief. He is not the least bit perturbed by his saturated condition.)

*(***EVA** *appears. She's wearing only a towel, having stepped fresh from the shower.)*

ALFRED. Oh, sorry. Hello.

EVA. Are you a pervert or something?

ALFRED. The door was open.

EVA. I'm kidding.

ALFRED. Oh.

(He laughs. He smiles.)

Sorry. I shouldn't have just barged in.

EVA. You're all wet.

ALFRED. Yes. *(pointing again to the doorway)* The um…Did I startle you? I'm really sorry.

EVA. That makes two of us.

ALFRED. You're sorry as well?

EVA. I'm wet as well. *(snaps her fingers)* Snap!

ALFRED. Pardon?

EVA. Snap!

It's a stupid game my brother and I played when we were kids. You know: if we *said* the same thing or *wore*

11

the same shirt or *did* the same thing at the same time. We'd go 'snap!'

(She snaps her fingers again.)

ALFRED. Oh. I see.

(He smiles.)

That sounds fun.

EVA. No, it's lame. Kids are lame.

ALFRED. *(Not necessarily agreeing)* Right.

(Beat.)

EVA. You have kids?

ALFRED. Yes. A daughter.

EVA. You don't look like a father.

ALFRED. Well, I am. She's fifteen. *(Enthusiastically)* Want to see a picture?

EVA. Not really.

(Beat. ALFRED looks around the apartment.)

ALFRED. Must have been nice.

EVA. Nice?

ALFRED. *(Smiling)* Growing up with a brother. I was an only child.

EVA. My brother's dead.

(ALFRED stops smiling.)

ALFRED. I'm sorry.

EVA. You didn't know him.

He threw himself from a hotel window.

A balcony overlooking the Winooski River, spring break of his senior year.

On account of a girl.

(Long pause. ALFRED is lost for what to say.)

ALFRED. Where exactly *is* the Winooski River?

(Pause.)

EVA. Who are you?

ALFRED. I'm early, aren't I?

EVA. Depends.

ALFRED. On what?

EVA. What were you expecting?

ALFRED. Eduardo?

EVA. *(Instant recognition; her demeanor changes.)* Oh, you're that *guy!*

ALFRED. Am I? That guy?

EVA. Albert.

ALFRED. Alfred.

EVA. Right!

ALFRED. Alfred Rehm. I'm a colleague? At the college. He said dinner Friday.

EVA. He did, did he?

ALFRED. I think so, yeah. It's Friday night, right?

EVA. Yeah, I dunno, I don't keep track.

(beat)

Dinner, huh? Well, I guess I have to pay my way somehow.

(She re-tucks her towel.)

ALFRED. Look, I can come back later.

EVA. You wanna drink?

(She heads to a drinks table and splashes some gin into two glasses.)

ALFRED. I think I'll wait until...

*(She returns, handing **ALFRED** the drink he didn't order.)*

EVA. Hope you like gin.

ALFRED. Fantastic.

EVA. There's no ice. I have sensitive teeth.

ALFRED. You're Eva, aren't you?

EVA. You tell me.

ALFRED. Eduardo told me there was someone new in his life.

EVA. I guess that would be me then, huh?

ALFRED. I guess.

EVA. Unless he's keeping secrets.

'Someone new in his life.' Is that what he said, Alfie?

ALFRED. That's what he said.

EVA. Sounds kinda temporary, doesn't it?

ALFRED. I think it sounds hopeful.

EVA. I'll guess we'll find out.

(*beat*)

ALFRED. Well, it's nice to meet you. Finally.

EVA. Is it?

(*pause*)

What's your daughter's name?

ALFRED. Claire.

(**EVA** *just stares at him.*)

(**ALFRED** *looks around the apartment at some of the sculptures, many in progress.*)

Looks like he's been busy.

EVA. Eduardo said you were married.

ALFRED. I am married.

EVA. You don't look married.

(**ALFRED** *holds up his hand comically, showing her his wedding ring.*)

ALFRED. Fourteen years.

EVA. What's that supposed to mean?

ALFRED. Nothing. Did Eduardo...?

EVA. How come she's not here?

ALFRED. Hmmn?

EVA. The wifey. Whatsername.

ALFRED. Oh, she um, Melinda, we took separate cars, she'll be here.

EVA. Belinda.

ALFRED. Melinda.

EVA. Are you sure?

ALFRED. *(smiling)* Pretty sure.

(weak attempt at humor) It has been fourteen years.

We took separate cars, we're breaking in a new babysitter, so...

EVA. I think Eduardo thinks her name's Belinda. You might wanna clarify that.

(ALFRED thinks he's supposed to laugh.)

ALFRED. Thanks. I will.

EVA. Babysitter? Thought you said your kid was fifteen?

ALFRED. Yes.

EVA. Your kid's fifteen and he still needs a babysitter?

ALFRED. *She.* She has some medical issues.

EVA. When I was fifteen I had a parole officer.

(He's not sure if she's joking.)

What kind of medical issues?

ALFRED. Did um, Eduardo say when he'd be back?

EVA. The conversation not scintillating enough for ya?

ALFRED. *(laughing)* No, no, I just meant, I could go, you know, and then come back when you're ready. I fear I arrived in the midst of...

(She smiles.)

EVA. Midst of what? What makes you think I'm not ready?

(EVA looks at ALFRED.)

ALFRED. Your towel for one thing.

EVA. Maybe I always entertain company in a towel. What do you think of that, mister?

What would you say...if I told you...I always entertain company in a towel?

(beat)

Hey, how tall are you?*

ALFRED. Sorry?

EVA. I thought you'd be taller.

ALFRED. No, I'm...this tall.

EVA. Yeah, when Eduardo said, "My friend Alfred Rehm and his wife might be coming for dinner," I don't know I just pictured this guy who was, you know...taller.

*(**ALFRED** sets down his briefcase.)*

(He stands as erect as possible.)

Is your wife tall?

ALFRED. Taller than me.

EVA. Well, that's probably why!

ALFRED. Why what?

EVA. Musta pictured Belinda.

ALFRED. Melinda.

EVA. That's what I said.

(She glares at him. He smiles.)

ALFRED. If you prefer I'll withdraw...

(She guffaws.)

What's funny?

EVA. Some of the things you say. "If you prefer I'll withdraw?" "I fear I arrived in the midst..." Yeah, I don't think people actually say things like that. I mean, do they?

ALFRED. Well, I just did, so...the evidence suggests...

EVA. See, there you go again: "the evidence suggests."

ALFRED. Well, perhaps you have a point.

---

*Please see the Appendix at the end of the script for alternate dialogue.

EVA. I do.

 I have lots of points.

 (She crosses to refill her glass. She also takes out a cigarette.)

 You smoke?

ALFRED. No.

EVA. Figgers!

ALFRED. Not since college, and then only at parties. When I was drunk. To impress girls.

 (He smiles dumbly. She stares at him.)

EVA. Stay there. I'll be right back.

 (She steps onto the fire escape.)

 (off) Eduardo gets pissed if I smoke inside. I've been banished to the fire escape.

ALFRED. Oh, no!

EVA. *(off)* I'm actually quitting.

ALFRED. Good for you.

EVA. *(off)* I'm doing pretty good, too.

ALFRED. You doing one of those patches?

EVA. *(off)* No, it's my own system. I started by limiting myself to three puffs per cigarette, then two, and now I'm down to one little puff. It's pretty affective.

ALFRED. Great, how long you been on the program?

EVA. *(off)* Four an' a half years.

 (She steps back in, blowing smoke out the door.)

 All done!

 You teach English, right?

ALFRED. Not really, I...

EVA. Eduardo said you were this great writer.

ALFRED. That's not accurate.

EVA. Got published in the *New York Times* and everything.

ALFRED. I wrote a few things. And it was *The New Yorker.*

EVA. What things?

ALFRED. A few short stories.

EVA. About what?

ALFRED. A long time ago.

Before I started teaching.

EVA. Teaching *English.*

ALFRED. Well, no, I teach French Literature, actually.

EVA. Sounds boring.

ALFRED. I enjoy it.

EVA. Oh, yeah?

ALFRED. Mostly 18th and 19th Century.

Dabble from time to time in some Post-War stuff.

EVA. Still sounds boring.

(beat)

So you speak French?

ALFRED. Well...

EVA. The last guy I lived with was bi-lingual.

ALFRED. Great.

EVA. But he was a dick.

He hit me once and I said 'If you touch me again I'll kill you' and I meant it too. He got all apologetic, like guys do, and sort of laughed it off, but I knew he would do it again. So when he went off to his shit job the next morning...?

ALFRED. *(slack-jawed)* Uhuh.

EVA. ...I poured lighter fluid all over his mattress and sheets and pillowcases and the sweats he slept in and when he flopped into bed that night, he was all, what the fuck is that smell? And I walked out of the bathroom, with my bags packed, a candle burning and I walked up to him, walked right up beside the bed and leaned in real close all sweet and sexy like and I said, 'I can either stay or go, stay or go, it's entirely up to you. What do you want me to do?'

*(She turns to **ALFRED**. Beat.)*

ALFRED. I'm not bilingual.

My French is...passable...at best.

EVA. I thought you said you teach French Literature?

ALFRED. I do teach French Literature.

EVA. How can you teach French Literature with passable French?

ALFRED. French Literature in *translation.*

EVA. Translation into what?

ALFRED. English.

EVA. So: you *do* teach English!

ALFRED. Ah, that's...another one of your points.

(simultaneously)

EVA....the point I was trying to make.

ALFRED. Snap!

*(**ALFRED** laughs at his own joke.)*

*(**EVA** looks at the floor where **ALFRED** is standing.)*

(There's a puddle forming.)

EVA. You want another drink?

ALFRED. I'm good.

(She pours him another drink anyway.)

EVA. You made a puddle on Eduardo's floor.

ALFRED. *(He hasn't noticed until now.)* Oh, god, I'm sorry, I've just been standing here like an idiot, chatting away, do you have anything to mop it up?

EVA. What like a towel or something?

*(**ALFRED** looks concernedly at her as she adjusts her towel.)*

I'm kidding. You should see your face.

Your eyes went like...

(She gives a moronic wide-eyed look.)

Take 'em off.

ALFRED. Excuse me?

EVA. Pants.

ALFRED. No, that's fine.

EVA. Come on, dummy, strip. I'll hang them over the vent, they'll be dry in no time. I don't want you sitting down to dinner in wet chinos. It'll fuck up the leather.

ALFRED. Well, I...

(She starts out.)

EVA. I'll grab you a pair of sweats or something.

*(**ALFRED** closes the front door and then sheepishly removes his wet slacks and socks. He keeps his boxers on self-consciously.)*

EVA. *(from off)* Hey, as long as you're here, what d'ya want for dinner? You don't have any allergies do you?

ALFRED. No. Anything's fine.

EVA. *(off)* What about Belinda?

ALFRED. Melinda.

EVA. *(off)* Right, what about her? She allergic?

ALFRED. Really, we'll eat just about anything, don't go to extremes.

EVA. *(off)* Extremes?
How about shish kebabs?

ALFRED. Great!

EVA. *(off)* We got a grill out on the fire escape.

ALFRED. You need any help?

EVA. *(off)* Yeah, we got a grill out on the fire escape.

ALFRED. Oh, okay, got it!

*(**ALFRED** exits briefly.)*

(off) Is there a trick to this?

EVA. *(off)* Yeah, you see the button?

ALFRED. *(off)* Uhuh.

EVA. *(off)* The red one?

ALFRED. *(off)* Okay?

EVA. *(off)* That says 'Push to start'?

ALFRED. *(off)* Yeah?

EVA. *(off)* That's the trick.

(We hear the 'click' as he starts the grill. He returns.)

ALFRED. It's all fired up.

EVA. *(off)* Thank god there's a man in charge.

(ALFRED laughs at himself.)

Eduardo went to get wine by-the-way. In case you're wondering where your bosom buddy went.

ALFRED. Oh, I brought some too.

(He unwraps his bottle of wine and places it on the drinks table.)

EVA. *(off)* I don't know why. He's got like three hundred bottles back here he's "saving for a special occasion" but no occasion ever seems special enough...

(EVA reenters in an oversized work shirt that obviously belongs to Eduardo and a pair of woolly and hideously colored socks. She has pair of Adidas tracksuit pants over her shoulder. She has lotion.)

(ALFRED can't help but look at her legs.)

EVA. *(cont.)*...so when he's at school I drink his good shit.

(She tosses ALFRED the towel she was just wearing. He begins to sop up the puddle he made.)

You're not gonna rat me out are you?

ALFRED. No. No, no, it'll be our little secret.

EVA. You promise?

ALFRED. I promise.   .

EVA. Swear?

ALFRED. I swear.

(She finally hands him the tracksuit pants. He goes back to cleaning his puddle. She applies lotion to her legs.)

EVA. Were you just looking at my legs?

ALFRED. I, sorry?

EVA. Were you: looking at my legs?

ALFRED....no, I, what?

EVA. Don't lie, Alfie.

ALFRED. I...I...

EVA. I'm kidding!!! You are so easy to get.

> (ALFRED *laughs.*)

> You were though, right?

> (ALFRED *stares at her.*)

> It's okay. I have nice legs. I'm not oblivious. You can tell me.

> (ALFRED *smiles awkwardly. Beat.*)

EVA. *(cont.)* You don't mention the wine, I don't mention the legs. Deal?

> (ALFREDS *nods.*)

How'd you get so wet anyhow?

ALFRED. Oh, yes, well, funny story, all that rain we had yesterday? I got here, I parked my car across from the pharmacist...

EVA. It rained yesterday?

ALFRED. Yeah, yes all day. All week, actually, there's been a deluge. You didn't notice?

EVA. I was asleep.

ALFRED. All week?

> (*She frowns at him and reclines on the couch with her gin.* ALFRED *finishes cleaning up the mess and stands shyly behind the couch.* EVA *makes no attempt to give him any 'privacy.' He turns upstage embarrassedly and sneaks his boxer shorts off before slipping on the track pants.*)

ALFRED. Anyway, I'm trying to cross at the corner by that pawn shop...and there's this puddle, I mean, I'm talking on the scale of Lake Superior...

EVA. Yeah, I sleep a lot okay? Is that a crime or something now?

(Beat. ALFRED resumes his story.)

ALFRED....and I think to myself, I can navigate around this, or leap over it, and as I'm assessing the most favorable route...this guy, this...

EVA. *(sits right up)* What guy?

ALFRED. This...I don't know, some guy in an SUV...he flies past and all I see is this wall of water, this *tsunami* about to engulf me. So.

EVA. Fucker!

ALFRED. Well, *he* didn't know...

EVA. Bullshit.

ALFRED. No.

EVA. Bullshit, I bet he gunned it, I bet he saw you standing there, a prime target, and I bet you anything that fucker gunned it right for that puddle.

ALFRED. I think it was an accident.

EVA. Yeah, right. What color was the SUV?

ALFRED. I don't know...

EVA. *(sotto voce)* That fucker!

ALFRED. I'm sure had he known what transpired he'd have felt terribly. I'm just happy my reflex was to back up. You know? If I hadn't stepped back from the curb like I did it would be more than my pants that are drenched. So: silver lining.

(She suddenly smiles and nods her head.)

EVA. Oh, right, that's right!

ALFRED. Hmm?

EVA. Makes sense.

ALFRED. What?

EVA. Eduardo told me that's how you were.

ALFRED. How am I?

EVA. Happy.

ALFRED. Happy?

EVA. You're happy. He said you were this really happy guy.

ALFRED. I am?

EVA. Like all the time. Like nothing bothers you. Like ever.

ALFRED. He said that? Eduardo...

EVA. 'He's a cheery fucker.' His *exact* words. *(imitating* **EDUARDO***)* You know in that *accent.*

> (**ALFRED** and **EVA** *for the first time exchange a shared laugh at* **EDUARDO** *'s expense.)*

ALFRED. Interesting.

I never really thought about it.

> *(He thinks about it:)*

I suppose I am fairly content.

EVA. No, he said it was more than that, more than content, he talked about you like it was...

ALFRED. What?

EVA. You know, like it was, like you were...

ALFRED. Uhuh?

EVA. I don't know...'freakishly happy'...

ALFRED. Freakish?

EVA. His words, not mine.

ALFRED. How can one be freakishly happy...?

EVA. That's exactly what I said.

ALFRED. That's funny. That's...that's funny, he said that?

EVA. And then goes, 'Happy in spite of everything.'

> *(She crosses for another drink.)*

Sure you don't want another drink?

> *(beat)*

ALFRED. In spite of everything?

That was the actual phrase?

Huh.

Weird.

(beat)

What do you think he meant by that?

EVA. Got me.

ALFRED. When was this?

EVA. Oh, he loves you, Alfie, don't worry about it.

ALFRED. I'm not worried, I just...*you* know...out of curiosity.

EVA. I guess you guys are pretty close, huh? He calls you his brother.

ALFRED. I think that's just his Cuban eccentricity.

EVA. He said you really saved his ass after his divorce.

ALFRED. He had a rough patch there for a while.

EVA. He talked about these little weekend trips you two would go on together. Little male getaways.

ALFRED. We did a few of those, yeah, years ago. It was fun.

EVA. *Man*cations. That's what you called 'em?

ALFRED. That's what *he* called them. That's ancient history.

EVA. Yeah, well he talks about it all the time. Said you really helped him out. You healed him. Just to be around someone who was so happy all the time, in spite of everything, it really helped him put his own shit in perspective.

ALFRED. Hmmn.

He said that?

EVA. He didn't mean anything by it, he was just filling me in on your...character, you know, giving me some background and stuff, in anticipation of our eventual meeting, I guess.

(beat)

You know, so I'd be prepared.

ALFRED. Prepared?

EVA. So it wouldn't be a surprise.

ALFRED. What?

Surprised by what?

EVA. So I wouldn't be put off by you.

ALFRED. I don't under...

EVA. Your demeanor?

ALFRED. No...what exactly?...I'm not exactly sure I'm
following the thread of your...

*(She has returned with the bottle of gin, and dribbles
some more into ALFRED's glass. He instinctively takes a
gulp and she dribbles in a little more, then returns to the
couch and nurses the remainder of the bottle.)*

Thanks for the pants by the way.

EVA. You're welcome.

Don't take this the wrong way.

ALFRED. Okay.

EVA. Alfred. I don't trust happy people.

I never have.

Eduardo knows this about me.

He was just being gallant.

ALFRED. *(vaguely)* Right.

EVA. I think they're phoney.

I think they're hiding something.

I think they're devious.

ALFRED. Devious?

EVA. I think *so.* Yeah.

ALFRED. *Happy* people are devious?

(She nods.)

EVA. They're lying to themselves, and everyone around
them. I only trust people who are unhappy. Authentic
people.

ALFRED. That's um...interesting philosophy.

(He smiles. He scratches his head.)

What are you doing with Eduardo then? *(laughs)*
Pardon my cheekiness.

EVA. Eduardo's not happy.

ALFRED. Eduardo's not happy?

EVA. Is that some strategy? Repeating what I say?

ALFRED. I'm confused.

EVA. Eduardo.

He's not happy, okay?

ALFRED. Yes he is.

EVA. Trust me, he's not.

ALFRED. Sure he had a dark spot, but that was years ago. Now he's one of the happiest people I know.

EVA. Prove it. Can you prove it?

ALFRED. He's got his work...

EVA. *(makes the sound of a game show buzzer)* Wrong answer!

ALFRED. ...he's highly respected in his field...

EVA. His *field?*

ALFRED. ...his paintings sell for big money, his son just had a baby. He's a grandfather now.

EVA. Big whoop!

That's not happy.

He's not happy. Ask him.

He's miserable.

ALFRED. He's got *you.*

EVA. I'm not happy.

Do I look happy?

ALFRED. You look fine.

EVA. I've been drinking gin all day.

(beat)

I don't know a single person that's not high that's happy.

Are you high, Alfred?

ALFRED. You mean *high* high?

Am I...?

No.

EVA. And yet you claim you're happy.

   (ALFRED *laughs.*)

   He laughs.

ALFRED. Well I am. So's my wife. We're very happy.

EVA. And I say you're not.

   And Eduardo feels the same way.

   (pause)

ALFRED. Don't be ridiculous.

   Don't be ridiculous.

EVA. You don't believe me? Ask him.

   When he comes through that door. Ask the man.

   (She stares at him.)

   (He gives a little laugh.)

   (He looks at his watch.)

EVA. *(cont.)* You like bell peppers?

ALFRED. Uhuh.

EVA. Those shish kebabs aren't gonna shish themselves.

   (EVA *exits.*)

   (ALFRED *stands there for a moment silently looking off in the direction she left.*)

   (*He crosses to the drinks table and begins to open the bottle of wine he brought.*)

ALFRED. *(calling off to her)* Melinda should be here any second.

EVA. *(from off)* Who?

ALFRED. Melinda.

   It's not that far of a drive.

   And there was plenty of parking right in front.

   I should probably warn her about that puddle though, right?

   And the puddle bandits.

   Preying on innocent victims.

(**ALFRED** *walks around the loft, looking at some of the sculptures.*)

Eduardo.

He's never said that to me before.

The happy thing.

Never mentioned anything of the kind to me before. Ever.

EVA. *(off)* Men don't tell other men what they're really thinking.

ALFRED. Yes they do.

  (beat)

  Why not?

EVA. *(off)* Do you?

ALFRED. We're very close.

EVA. *(off)* That wasn't the question.

ALFRED. We've been friends for years.

EVA. *(off, prophetically)* Fourteen years!

  Onions okay?

ALFRED. How long have you been together?

EVA. *(off)* A month, ten days, half-hour, what does it matter?

ALFRED. Out of curiosity.

EVA. *(off)* That killed the cat, didn't it?

ALFRED. Why would he confide something like that to you and not to me?

EVA. *(poking her head briefly back into the room)* You're not fucking him.

  (**EVA** *disappears again.*)

  (**ALFRED** *takes a sip of wine, as...*)

  (**EDUARDO** *pushes energetically through the door, with baguettes and several bottles of wine tucked under both arms.*)

  (*His energy and charisma is instantly enchanting, and we should never for a moment wonder why such a young woman as* **EVA** *is living with him. His hair is wild, and* *he is unshaven. He wears a ridiculously brightly colored scarf, which he never takes off, and a ratty t-shirt under a very expensive full-length camel hair topcoat. He is limping.)*

EDUARDO. Hello brother!

ALFRED. Hi stranger.

EDUARDO. Come here you fucker!

*(**EDUARDO** wraps **ALFRED** in a bread and wine bottle embrace and kisses him on both cheeks.)*

EDUARDO. *(calling off)* Honey, I'm home! *(to **ALFRED**)* I like to say that. It's our little joke. *(Re: a bottle)* Grab that. Get the door, can you?

*(**ALFRED** relieves him of one of the bottles, closes the door.)*

*(**EDUARDO** crosses to the bar to set down the bottles of wine and baguettes. **ALFRED** notices his limp.)*

ALFRED. Are you okay? What happened?

EDUARDO. Some asshole tried to run me down in the street.

ALFRED. What?

EDUARDO. I memorized his plate number, I see this bastard again, I kick out his taillights.

*(**EDUARDO** records the plate numbers in his smartphone, and finally sits.)*

This neighborhood. I fucking love it.

Great spaces.

Shit neighbors.

Two years from now it'll be hip to live here and there'll be a Starbucks and tapas bar on every corner. For now, we have to be vigilant.

*(He suddenly looks at **ALFRED** as if for the first time.)*

Look at you! Your stupid face!

It's good to see you, man. How long has it been?

ALFRED. Too long.

EDUARDO. Come here you fucker!

(**EDUARDO** *rises; his ankle gives him some trouble.*)

ALFRED. Oh my god. You should ice that.

EVA. *(off)* Hey, is that my lover returned?

EDUARDO. It's Eduardo.

EVA. *(off)* Oh, okay, let me know when my lover returns.

EDUARDO. This is her joke every day. She's crazy, I love it. Sorry I abandoned you, we needed wine. And this bread, I had to get this bread, smell this bread.

(**EDUARDO** *sticks the baguette right under* **ALFRED**'s *nose.*)

ALFRED. It's fine, don't worry about it.

EDUARDO. No, it's amazing, right?

ALFRED. Yeah, wow, it is good.

EDUARDO. This Armenian guy.

ALFRED. Your ankle?

EDUARDO. Little family bakery, it's ten blocks, but worth every step, I need a drink. You want a drink? So, did you meet Eva?

ALFRED. Yes, we um...I did.

(**EDUARDO** *limps over to the drinks table, pours himself a glass of wine.*)

EDUARDO. *(He calls off.)* Eva, I got the wine!

EVA. *(off)* We didn't need wine, d'you get bread?

EDUARDO. I got bread!

ALFRED. Is your ankle okay? Do you need some ice or something?

EDUARDO. There is no ice on the premises. She has sensitive teeth.

So what are you drinking?

ALFRED. I had some gin. I brought some wine.

EDUARDO. So what do you think?

ALFRED. I prefer the wine.

EDUARDO. No, stupido. Eva. What do you think? She's great, no?

ALFRED. She's great.

EDUARDO. *(conspiratorially)* She has a tattoo.

(*beat*)

Where's your wife?

ALFRED. Running late.

EDUARDO. She needs to meet Eva.

They're so alike.

(**ALFRED** *doesn't think so.*)

They'll be great friends. Like us.

They can have lunches together.

They can walk through museums.

It'll be fantastic.

Eva doesn't have any friends.

ALFRED. Really.

EDUARDO. It's weird, because she's so...accessible, you know?

So she better show up.

ALFRED. She'll be here.

EDUARDO. I've been telling Eva all about her.

ALFRED. Yeah?

EDUARDO. How she's starting her own company now you've got in-home care. What is it again?

ALFRED. Promotional items.

EDUARDO. Right!

ALFRED. Listen Eduardo...

EDUARDO. Pens, refrigerator magnets...

ALFRED. She didn't seem to know.

About Claire.

Asking me questions like she had no idea, you know?

EDUARDO. She was being polite.

Of course I told her.

Or maybe...maybe she's unsure of how to approach the subject.

She doesn't know you.

(EDUARDO *walks* ALFRED *out of earshot of* EVA.)

But honestly, brother. What you think of her? It's important to me. I have these feelings, you know?

These deep feelings.

It's fucking weird.

It's been a long time.

And I swore to myself...

I value and trust your opinion in all things, so whatever you got to say.

(*pause*)

ALFRED. I just met her

EDUARDO. (*laughing*) Me too!

Seriously!

I don't think it's even a month!

ALFRED. (*not a question, an observation*) And she's moved in already.

EDUARDO. Isn't that great?

(*like it's some grand philosophical statement:*)

I mean, there was this moment...when she *wasn't* here, and then she *was* here, and everything just made sense, you know?

(ALFRED *doesn't know.*)

ALFRED. How old is she?

EDUARDO. Hhhmm?

ALFRED. Out of curiosity.

(EDUARDO *has never actually considered this question.*)

(*He considers the question:*)

EDUARDO. I don't know.

ALFRED. You don't know?

EDUARDO. It never came up.

ALFRED. The topic never...?

EDUARDO. We talk of other things.
Life. The universe.

(**EDUARDO** *looks at* **ALFRED**.)

(*pause*)

(*calling off*) Eva?

EVA. (*off*) Is that my lover calling?

EDUARDO. It's Eduardo.

EVA. (*off*) Oh, you're still here?

EDUARDO. I'm still here.

EVA. (*off*) Don't let my lover find out. He's insanely jealous.

EDUARDO. I have a question:

EVA. (*off*) So do I:

EDUARDO. You go first.

EVA. (*off*) Is Alfred a vegetarian?

ALFRED. I'm not a vegetarian.

EDUARDO. He's not a vegetarian.

EVA. (*off*) What about his wife?

EDUARDO. What about your wife?

ALFRED. She's not either.

EVA. (*off*) What did he say?

EDUARDO. They're both carnivores.

EVA. (*off*) Okay your turn.

EDUARDO. Hold old are you?

EVA. (*off*) Twenty-two.

EDUARDO. She's twenty-two.

(**ALFRED** *nods.*)

(**EDUARDO** *considers* **EVA**'s *age for first time.*)

(*Then he suddenly notices the track pants* **ALFRED**'s *wearing.*)

EDUARDO. Hey. Are you wearing my pants?

(**EVA** *enters.*)

(Both men stare at her.)

(She is now dressed in a very tight, very sexy, but very elegant cocktail dress. She looks entirely different than she did at the start of the play. Her makeup and hair is totally Goth.)

EDUARDO. Ay, Dios mio! You look amazing.

EVA. I know.

EDUARDO. Come here.

EVA. Say please.

EDUARDO. Come here, *please.*

(She walks over to him very slowly.)

Kiss me.

EVA. Beg me.

EDUARDO. I beg you!

EVA. Beg me some more.

EDUARDO. I beg you some more.

(They kiss.)

(It's a long one.)

(ALFRED *watches them, then gets uncomfortable.)*

(He drinks.)

*(***EDUARDO** *pulls away.)*

EDUARDO. *(cont.)* You've been smoking.

EVA. No I haven't.

EDUARDO. I can taste it.

EVA. I had one puff.

EDUARDO. Did you smoke inside?

EVA. *(Shakes her head)* Uh-uhn.

EDUARDO. Are you lying to me?

EVA. I don't lie.

Ask Alfie.

(EDUARDO *looks at* **ALFRED.***)*

(pause)

(We hear a knock at the door, and then from off, a tremulous voice:)

MELINDA. *(off)* Guys? Hello?

EDUARDO. There she is!

ALFRED. Come in, honey

MELINDA. *(off)* I'm sorry, I know I'm late.

EDUARDO. Get in here.

> **(MELINDA** *appears.)*
>
> *(She is absolutely drenched from head to foot.)*
>
> *(She is clutching what must have been a lovely bouquet of fresh flowers, which is now quite droopy and bedraggled. She stands, herself droopy and bedraggled, in the entryway.)*

MELINDA. Hello.

ALFRED. Oh, my god!

MELINDA. Could I bother you for a towel?

EVA. *(snapping her fingers)* Snap!!!

> *(blackout)*

TWO

(A few minutes later.)

*(**MELINDA** is in the bathroom. We can hear a blow-dryer going. **ALFRED** is trying to arrange the bedraggled flowers in a vase. **EDUARDO** is setting out plates and pouring wine.)*

EDUARDO. This prick.

ALFRED. Eduardo...

EDUARDO. This prick's been terrorizing the neighborhood for weeks.

ALFRED. She didn't say it was a black SUV.

EDUARDO. How much you wanna bet?

ALFRED. ...and even if it *was*...

EDUARDO. ...I'll put money on it. You wanna put money on it?

ALFRED. ...you know how many black SUVs are on the road?

EDUARDO. How many?

(beat)

ALFRED. Okay I don't have a *figure* for you...

EDUARDO. I'm telling you, it's the same guy. A skinny fucker.

ALFRED. You're funny, you know that?

EDUARDO. Skinny fucker with a floppy hat. He got you, he tried to get me and now he's assaulted your wife.

ALFRED. Assaulted? We got splashed with dirty rain water, not robbed at knife-point.

*(**EVA** enters with a sizzling plate of shish kebabs still on the skewers.)*

It's a coincidence.

EVA. Bullshit.

ALFRED. And I think 'terrorizing' is an overstatement. That looks delicious, Eva.

EVA. Thanks Alfie.

EDUARDO. The guy who nailed you, was he wearing a hat? Think!

ALFRED. I have no idea. I didn't see what he looked like.

EDUARDO. Think!

EVA. Was he tall or short?

ALFRED. I didn't see what he looked like.

EVA. He was short, right? Slinking behind the wheel.

(**MELINDA** *appears wearing a plush bathrobe. Her hair is 'poofy'.*)

MELINDA. Hey, guys, sorry.

EDUARDO. Dinner's ready.

MELINDA. Wonderful.

ALFRED. Hi, sweetheart, you okay?

MELINDA. I'm fine now. Thanks.

EVA. Nice hair.

(**MELINDA** *and* **ALFRED** *both laugh as* **MELINDA** *pats her hair down.*)

MELINDA. Oh, gosh, how embarrassing. Is it all sticking up? I'd just had it done, too.

EVA. Want some product?

MELINDA. No.

EVA. I can fix it up. My mom was a stylist.

(**EVA** *exits.*)

MELINDA. No, it's no bother.

ALFRED. It looks fine.

MELINDA. Seriously, I'll be fine. I'll just try not to call too much attention to myself for the remainder of the evening.

(**MELINDA** *laughs at her own joke, then notices the flowers drooping in their vase.*)

Oh dear. Sorry about the flowers. I don't think they're going to make it.

(**EVA** *returns with some hair goop. She situates herself behind* **MELINDA** *on the couch, sort of straddling her.*)

EVA. Scootch forward. Keep still.

MELINDA. Oh, okay.

Thanks for the robe, by the way. This is really soft *(to* **ALFRED***)* feel this *(to* **EVA***)* where did you get this?

EVA. At a store.

(**EVA** *starts applying product to Melinda's hair.*)

ALFRED. Your color's coming black. I was worried. You were blue.

MELINDA. My teeth were chattering while I was drying my hair.

EDUARDO. We heard.

(*simultaneously*)

ALFRED. We heard.

EDUARDO. *(pushing her wine glass toward her)* Here get this down you.

MELINDA. Thanks.

I always think of my childhood when my teeth chatter.

EVA. Why?

MELINDA. You know. Little kids.

EVA. No. Why?

MELINDA. They seem impervious to the cold when they're out tearing around having fun. The minute they come through that door, their little teeth start chattering and they can't stop. And it's very funny.

EVA. Do you have kids?

(**ALFRED** *looks at* **EVA.***)

MELINDA. Yes. Yes we do. Just one.

EVA. Do his teeth chatter?

MELINDA. Her. We have a daughter.

EVA. That's cool.

MELINDA. Her name's Claire.

ALFRED. *(smiling)* I told you that.

EVA. Did you? Shit, I'm sorry.

EDUARDO. She's forgetful.

EVA. I was discombobulated. Alfred surprised me in the shower.

> *(**EDUARDO** pops a cork on another bottle.)*

> *(**MELINDA** looks at **ALFRED**.)*

MELINDA. What...?

EVA. I'm kidding.

> *(**EVA** tilts **MELINDA**'s head up to sculpt her bangs.)*

Chin up. You've actually got great hair.

MELINDA. Oh, thanks.

EVA. You just don't wear it in a cut that's particularly flattering.

> *(pause)*

MELINDA. I left my wet things in the tub if that's okay.

EVA. You should go shorter. Accentuate your features.

MELINDA. It's always been this length.

EVA. That's what I'm saying. It's like you're hiding behind all this *length*. Who does your hair?

MELINDA. There's a woman I've...

> *(**EVA** stands.)*

EVA. She sucks. I could do it right now if you want.

MELINDA. What?

EVA. Cut your hair.
Right now.
Bring you up to date.

MELINDA. No, no really, I...

EVA. *(heading off)* It'll be fun.

    (pause)

EDUARDO. How's the wine?

MELINDA. Delicious, thanks. *(re: the food)* And look at this?

    (EVA returns with scissors.)

ALFRED. It smells amazing, Eva.

EDUARDO. This one can cook.

EVA. I do what I'm told.

    That's why he keeps me around.

    They all laugh at her joke, hoping it's a joke.

    (EVA crosses to MELINDA and takes a length of her hair in her fingers.)

    You ready?

MELINDA. You don't have to, seriously.

EVA. It's no big deal. Hold still, I don't wanna knick ya.

MELINDA. Why don't we eat first?

EVA. Ya sure?

ALFRED. Yeah, yeah.

    (beat)

EVA. It's your head, I guess.

EDUARDO. Yeah, everyone grab a plate, what you do is...

    (They do. EVA just watches them.)

MELINDA. ...just grab a fork...

ALFRED. Okay.

    (begin overlapping dialogue:)

EDUARDO. You take a fork and scrape it off the thing onto your plate. Here's a plate.

MELINDA. Thanks, like this?

ALFRED. Oh, my god...

MELINDA. I know.

EDUARDO. What did I tell you?

ALFRED. ...these mushrooms, look at the size of them.

MELINDA. I'm actually drooling.

EDUARDO. I know!

MELINDA. Look at me.

ALFRED. She is. She's officially drooling.

MELINDA. I am starving. I skipped lunch, which is never a good idea. I get jittery. Did you try the shrimp?

ALFRED. I *proposed* to the shrimp.

EDUARDO. *(his mouth full of shrimp)* The shrimp, the shrimp!

(end overlapping dialogue)

(a brief pause while they're all chewing, then…)

MELINDA. Eva, you're not eating?

EVA. I'm drinking.

(She pours herself another gin.)

EDUARDO. She does this.

EVA. No I don't.

EDUARDO. She does, she stays home all day.

EVA. He's lying.

EDUARDO. Doesn't touch a thing. Then she'll whip up this amazing meal. She pretends like it's such a pain in the ass.

EVA. It *is* a pain in the ass.

EDUARDO. She jokes.

EVA. It's a pain when I don't know you've invited guests over.

EDUARDO. She knew, I told her.

EVA. No he didn't.

ALFRED. You told me he told you.

EVA. I told you lots of things.

EDUARDO. Honey!

EVA. He never tells me anything.

He likes to spring things on me.

He likes to see how I react.

He's sadistic.

EDUARDO. She's joking.

But she will: she'll cook this extraordinary food, steamed oysters and stuffed quail, gazpacho, steaks... and not touch a bite. I'll have to sit here and watch *her* watch *me* eat it all by myself. And get fat.

EVA. I like you fat. Makes me look thinner.

EDUARDO. Then I fall asleep on the couch, and I'll wake up at two-three in the morning and there she is, alone in the dark, with a jar of peanut butter and a spoon. Gorging herself. Right? Right?

*(**ALFRED** smiles.)*

*(**MELINDA** smiles.)*

*(**EDUARDO** playfully kisses **EVA** on the cheek.)*

EDUARDO. *(cont.)* I'd like to propose a toast.

(They all take up their glasses.)

ALFRED. Can I do the honors?

To your new grandson.

MELINDA. Yes.

EDUARDO. Thank you.

ALFRED. To the two of you.

And to my wonderful wife, and her exciting new business venture.

MELINDA. That's so sweet.

EVA. What's this?

MELINDA. It's nothing, a little concern

ALFRED. No, no, it's a big deal, it is. *(to **EVA**)* Well, Eduardo told you already.

*(**EDUARDO**, **ALFRED** and **MELINDA** clink glasses. **EVA** just sits there.)*

EVA. No. What?

*(**ALFRED** looks at **EDUARDO**.)*

MELINDA. *(very excited to share)* I'm starting my own company. I think that's the first time I've announced it publicly. Aaagh! I was at the hospital and I went into the gift shop for something and there were all these key chains and little flashlights and balloons and all sorts of things with the name of the hospital and it occurred to me, someone made those, someone *sold* those, I spend a lot of time around hospitals, and I'm a people person to boot, so why couldn't I do the same thing. Promotional items. A niche. So I did a little research and voila. That gift shop was my first account and now I have seven or eight and not just hospitals either, I have a car dealership and a hairdresser, funnily enough, and business, as they say, is booming.

EVA. Well, shit, congratulations. I wish I'd known. I'd have had a cake or a card or something.

(*EVA smacks* EDUARDO *on the arm, quite hard.*)

(*They all eat in silence for a few moments. Just the sound of the forks clinking on the plates, the 'tink' of wine glasses.*)

(*EVA sips her gin.*)

(*We hear a police siren off in the distance.* EVA *looks off toward the fire escape.*)

EVA. I think it's a sign. I think it means something.

ALFRED. What's a sign?

EVA. A portent of things to come.

EDUARDO. Baby, what are you talking about?

EVA. Just now?
    The car?
    That drenched you?
    It was an SUV, right?

MELINDA. It happened so fast. I'd be hopeless as an eye witness.

(*She laughs. She puts food in her mouth.*)

EVA. Do you remember the color?

EDUARDO. Of the SUV. Was it...?

EVA. Don't tell her.

(*Beat. They wait a moment for* **MELINDA** *to finish chewing her food and swallow it.*)

MELINDA. It was black.

I think.

It *could* have been black, it was dark.

There's not much light on that corner.

But I think black.

EDUARDO. Same guy.

MELINDA. I do remember this hat.

These peppers are delicious.

He...I think it was a he...he had on this funny hat.

EDUARDO. What did I tell you?

MELINDA. What?

ALFRED. They've got a conspiracy theory going.

Eduardo thinks it was the same guy who splashed me.

EVA. Because it was.

(**MELINDA** *laughs.*)

MELINDA. Now that would be funny.

ALFRED. A rogue element in the neighborhood. Bent on soaking all of humanity.

(**EDUARDO** *tracks down his cell phone.*)

EDUARDO. I got his plates right here. Smart Phone, baby!

(*He shows* **MELINDA**.)

EVA. We should call the cops.

ALFRED. Yes, that's it, call the cops: "Hello, I'd like to report a dousing!"

(**MELINDA** *laughs.*)

EDUARDO. The cops won't do anything. I'll take care of this myself.

MELINDA. Eduardo!

ALFRED. Who are you, Charles Bronson?

EDUARDO. If it was *your* neighborhood...

ALFRED. A puddle. A splash. A change of clothes. We shouldn't let it ruin our evening.

MELINDA. I agree. We haven't had lots of these. Nights out. Let's forget about it. It was an accident, obviously. We've had lots of rain. I'm just happy to be here. I'm happy to be dry again. I'm really happy about this wine.

EDUARDO. Another glass?

MELINDA. I probably shouldn't. Just a drop.

EVA. Was he tall or short, do you remember?

The guy, the SUV, tall like Eduardo or short like Alfie?

EDUARDO. A skinny fucker?

ALFRED. Aren't we supposed to be having fun?

MELINDA. It *is* fun. This is funny.

EVA. You guys are funny.

(ALFRED *and* MELINDA *stare at her.*)

Nothing pisses you off.

MELINDA. What do you mean?

EVA. This should piss you off. You should be totally pissed off. It's weird. Nothing pisses you off.

MELINDA. I wish that were true.

EVA. *Nothing.*

ALFRED. Not this. Other things.

EVA. What things?

MELINDA. Serious things.

EVA. For instance?

MELINDA. Well...

Things...

EVA. Uhuh?

ALFRED. Things...which are not...ostensibly...frivolous.

(EVA *laughs quite loudly.*)

Silver lining: no one got hurt.

Now can we please change the subject.

MELINDA. *(a little ritual, a little mantra)* Yes: I close my eyes. *(She closes her eyes.)* I open my eyes. *(She does.)* There. All gone, all better.

(EVA *stares at* MELINDA.)

(ALFRED *goes to one of the statues while pouring himself a glass.* EVA *grabs another cigarette.*)

EVA. I'm having a smoke.

EDUARDO. Fire escape!

EVA. *(To* MELINDA*)* Wanna join me?

MELINDA. I don't smoke, thanks.

EVA. Alfie said you did.

ALFRED. No I didn't.

EVA. In college.

MELINDA. No.

EVA. Not often. At parties.

MELINDA. Not ever.

ALFRED. That was me.

EVA. Oh.

MELINDA. What? I didn't know that.

ALFRED. *(re: sculpture)* Eduardo. Tell me about this. I'm curious about this. This new stuff, it looks fascinating. I've never seen you work in this medium before.

MELINDA. Yes, it's terrifically...err...what's the word I'm looking for?

EVA. *(as she heads to the fire escape)* Ugly?

MELINDA. Arresting.

EDUARDO. It's not me.

ALFRED. What?

EDUARDO. This is Eva's work.

MELINDA. Oh.

ALFRED. Really?

MELINDA. Very impressive.

ALFRED. *(calling off)* I didn't know you were an artist, Eva.

EVA. *(off)* You didn't ask.

EDUARDO. Isn't it great?

ALFRED. Wow, it's wonderful.

MELINDA. What's it made of? Is that...?

EVA. *(off)* It's junk. It's garbage, scrap.

MELINDA. You're kidding, this is all...?

> *(**EVA** re-enters, blowing smoke off, and slumps down beside **MELINDA** on the couch.)*

EVA. Do you have any photos of your son?

EDUARDO. Daughter.

EVA. Do you have any photos of your daughter?

MELINDA. Oh. Yes. Yes, I do. Would you like to see?

EVA. I would.

> *(**MELINDA** takes her phone from her purse.)*

> *(**ALFRED** drifts back over to the couch and **MELINDA**.)*

MELINDA. That's Claire.

EVA. Oh.

> *(She examines the picture in great detail.)*

She's just a little bitty thing.

> *(**EVA** nods.)*

> *(**EDUARDO** looks at **ALFRED**.)*

How old is she?

MELINDA. Fifteen. *(re: photo)* But this is Sedona, so, we went there...was it two years ago?

> *(**ALFRED** nods.)*

So she's thirteen. In this.

This is...it's hard to tell from this but it's a...well they call them healing vortexes. The energy of the universe is supposed to swirl around and converge right here on the summit...according to the Chamber of Commerce, anyway. People from all over the world make pilgrimages to these red rocks. It took us forever to carry Claire up to the top and Alfred got terrible sunstroke that day, didn't you Alfred?

(ALFRED nods.)

And there was this really annoying man, remember? At the top. With his geriatric mother shouting into his cell phone...I thought that was very rude. We were all trying to bask in the serenity and he was disrupting whatever curative energy might have been available at the time, so you ask if nothing pisses me off? That did.

(beat)

EVA. What's wrong...?

MELINDA. What's wrong with her?

EVA. No...

MELINDA. It's okay. I'm not embarrassed to talk about it, she's my daughter. She has Cerebral Palsy.

EVA. That's...

MELINDA. No, it's not hard, it's easy, it's the easiest thing in the world. This is our daughter, this is the reality, she's different, you adapt, I can't envision our lives being any other way, can you?

(ALFRED moves away.)

I credit Alfred. He has more patience than I do. Especially in the beginning, it was very frustrating, and I would come to the end of my tether some days. But Alfred, he's...there's this lightness to everything, he...he's never lost his temper with Claire ever, never expressed any...

(She looks at her husband; points at him.)

Him: right there. Alfred has single-handedly read our daughter the bulk of the classics of Western Literature. Of course he's admittedly partial to the Frogs.

(She laughs.)

But you name it, Alfred's read it to her. Joyce, Flaubert, Hugo, Dickens. Hours at a stretch, hours. Our daughter is more well-read than most people I know.

If we could see inside her mind, you know, if we could just climb into her head we'd find all these wonderful worlds sloshing around, all these extraordinary lives, this landscape of possibilities. That's Alfred.

There's no denying it was hard at first. *(to* **ALFRED***)* You were trying to focus on your writing back then, which, I think it's fair to say, took a back seat. Is that fair to say? But now ... we have our routines. We have structure. We have in-home care, so Alfred's started writing again, and I'm going back to work, and we can actually come out once in a while and get a little drunk and giddy with our old friends. And our new ones.

(She very formally holds her glass up to **EDUARDO** *and then* **EVA***, and drinks to them. Pause.)*

EVA. I wasn't asking what was wrong with Claire.

MELINDA. Oh.

What were you asking?

EVA. Something else.

It doesn't matter.

(pause)

Alfred writes? You write? I didn't know that.

EDUARDO. He's a wonderful writer. I told you this.

EVA. Anything I would have seen?

MELINDA. Well...

EVA. Like movies, or...?

EDUARDO. Short stories.

MELINDA. My favorite was a story in *The New Yorker* the year before we got married.

ALFRED. No one's interested.

MELINDA. "The Somnambulist." It was about this man, well a kid, really, who...walks in his sleep.

EVA. Walks in his sleep!

MELINDA. Yes!

EDUARDO. You know, maybe you've had too much gin, Eva. I told her all about this.

EVA. No he didn't.

I wish you'd stop making me sound like a total flake.

EDUARDO. I'll get you some water.

EVA. What are you, my father?

(an uncomfortable silence)

MELINDA. Alfred, you should give her a copy. It's my absolute favorite of his, he walks in his sleep and there's hours at a time totally unaccounted for, and these hours turn into days, and he has no idea where he goes or what he does, and his girlfriend...it's his girlfriend, right? His girlfriend starts following him one night, and, and...I won't spoil it for you, would you like me to send you a copy?

EVA. Not really.

MELINDA. Oh.

EVA. I don't have time to sit around and read. I'm too busy forgetting shit Eduardo told me. Apparently.

EDUARDO. Hey.

(pause)

ALFRED. *(to the rescue)* Well, I'm interested in Eva's sculpture, that's what I want to talk about.

MELINDA. I'm sorry, that was rude of me to high-jack the conversation. I do that sometimes. I high-jack. I embroider. I assume people want more details than it turns out they actually want or need. I'll shut up and drink my wine.

ALFRED. Eduardo, walk us through this.

EVA. *(to EDUARDO)* What, are you sulking now?

(EDUARDO, though still wounded, acquiesces.)

EDUARDO. For someone who never had any formal training, it's remarkable. Not just the craftsmanship, but the *thought* behind it. Not only do you engage the work with your eyes, but...it's more visceral than that. You want to touch it, it invites you to touch it. And Eva's going to print little permission notices on cardstock that say: "Go ahead. It's okay. Touch it." It really fucks

with the viewer, you see, who's accustomed to keeping
their hands off the art, right? It's transgressive.

(Pause. They all look at the work.)

EVA. Do you like it?

ALFRED. It's striking.

EVA. I'll ask someone else. *(to* **MELINDA***)* Do you like it?
Would you buy it?

*(***MELINDA** *laughs a little uncomfortably.)*

MELINDA. I'm not sure where we'd put it. We don't have a
lot of room.

EVA. Would you buy it for a friend?

MELINDA. It's hard to know people's tastes.

ALFRED. Art is so subjective, isn't it?

EVA. I don't know what that even means. I don't understand
either of you. You're totally cryptic. More wine?

MELINDA. Err, please. Just a...

*(***EVA** *pours* **MELINDA***'s wine. She fills it up right to the
top.)*

Thanks.

EDUARDO. I instantly recognized her talent.

EVA. Before or after we slept together?

EDUARDO. Ha-ha!
She did a show last month with a couple of other artists
and I attended.

MELINDA. And that's how you met?

EDUARDO. That's how we met.

MELINDA. How fun!

EVA. We met at a club. The lame-o followed me from the
gallery to a club. *Stalked*, more like.

EDUARDO. Guilty.

*(***ALFRED** *laughs.)*

EVA. He was really drunk and stupid and way too attentive.

EDUARDO. A searing but accurate portrait.

EVA. ...wanted to talk about *the work*, which was cute, but I was like, "You don't have to be so obvious, I've already decided I'm going home with you, if you keep talking it's just going to boomerang on you."

EDUARDO. So I shut up.

ALFRED. Of course you did.

MELINDA. That's a really cute story.

(**ALFRED** *inspects a second sculpture.*)

ALFRED. So, Eva?

EVA. Yes, Alfie?

ALFRED. So is this a series?

EVA. I guess.

EDUARDO. She hates talking about her work. I'm encouraging her to get better at articulating what she's attempting to do.

EVA. Does anyone want dessert? I got pie.

EDUARDO. Avoiding dialogue about the work is a form of aesthetic arrogance.

(**EVA** *blows him a big kiss as she exits.*)

People want to know what going on inside the work, inside the mind of the creator –

EVA. No they don't.

ALFRED & MELINDA. Yes we do!

(**EDUARDO** *picks back up with:*)

EDUARDO. It implicates them (in a good way) in the creative process...it helps them develop an appreciation for art in general by getting closer to understanding one piece in particular.

(**EVA** *returns with an apple pie.*)

But she hates this shit.

EVA. He's right, I hate this shit, who wants pie?

MELINDA. Me please.

EVA. It's just apple.

MELINDA. My favorite. Is there ice cream?

EVA. Nope.

EDUARDO. She has sensitive teeth.

MELINDA. Oh, I'm sorry, I know that can be awful. But there's toothpaste now, my sister actually...

EVA. We all have our crosses to bear.

Sensitive teeth.

Chattering teeth.

Other *serious* things.

Things which are not ostensibly...frivolous.

(beat)

Pie?

ALFRED. What's the subject? If you don't mind. I'm curious.

EVA. The subject.

ALFRED. If you had to describe it.

EVA. You mean, like at gunpoint?

EDUARDO. Come on!

ALFRED. Is there a theme that connects these pieces?

EVA. Not really.

EDUARDO. Don't be coy.

EVA. Oh, I was going for disinterested, did it come across as coy?

EDUARDO. Go on, tell them. They're interested.

EVA. They're just being polite.

MELINDA. No, no...

EDUARDO. You've been working on this for a while now. Eva, don't be so close-lipped about the work. Our friends want to share in your process.

*(**ALFRED** moves closer to the one sculpture that remains draped in a tarp.)*

ALFRED. What's this one?

(**ALFRED** *starts to remove the tarp.* **EVA** *suddenly jumps up.*)

EVA. DON'T FUCKING TOUCH THAT!

ALFRED. Sorry. I. Sorry.

EVA. It's not ready yet.

(*beat*)

EDUARDO. The subject is happiness.

MELINDA. Happiness?

EDUARDO. She's trying to find where it's located in the human body. Because it's rarely depicted anywhere other than the face.

MELINDA. (*a mouthful of pie*) I never thought about that.

EDUARDO. So: this is the work.

EVA. I really wish you would stop saying "the work", it's fucking annoying.

(*Silence. Everyone looks at their drinks, the floor.*)

Sorry I yelled at you, Alfie.

ALFRED. Actually...

Do you mind if I politely ask you not to call me that?

EVA. Call you what?

ALFRED. Alfie.

Not to be rude.

EVA. You don't like it?

ALFRED. I prefer Alfred.

EVA. You do?

ALFRED. I do.

MELINDA. No one calls him that.

ALFRED. If you don't mind.

MELINDA. Except his father.

ALFRED. Sweetheart.

MELINDA. But he did it because he knew Alfred hated it.

EVA. What a dick!

EDUARDO. Eva.

ALFRED. Well, it's just not my name. That's all. That's all. My name's Alfred. So. It's not a big deal.

(**EVA** *stops serving pie and stands looking solemnly at* **ALFRED**.)

(*silence*)

EVA. Okay.

I thought it was cute.

My bad.

I thought...

I know you're Eduardo's best friend.

I was trying to feel close to you.

I meant it as an endearment.

I was nervous to meet you.

You guys are like brothers and who am I?

It took me forever to figure out what to wear, what to cook.

I wasn't even ready when you got here, because I was so...aaggghh!!! You know? Okay. I get it.

I just...never...quite know what to...*do*...around people.

I'm stupid.

I fucking hate myself.

I need a smoke.

(**MELINDA** *and* **ALFRED** *stare at each other, slack-jawed. They have no idea how to react, no idea if she's being sincere or not.*)

(**EVA** *slowly crosses to the drinks table to refill her glass, then starts to head off toward the fire escape.*)

ALFRED. Eva.

(**EVA** *stops, turns back.*)

It's okay, I'm sorry...

I, um...I didn't...

EVA. What?

ALFRED. I thought you were...

EVA. Look, maybe I should hit the hay.

MELINDA. No.

ALFRED. It's fine, forget it.

EVA. What?

ALFRED. Seriously. I don't know why I got so...

My dad *was* kind of a dick.

(He laughs.)

It's just a name. I shouldn't be so sensitive. Forget it.

EVA. Yeah?

*(**ALFRED** nods.)*

So...is it okay? I mean...

ALFRED. Uhum.

EVA. Really?

ALFRED. We're good.

EVA. If I...?

ALFRED. What?

EVA. If I call you Alfie? Still?

*(Pause. **EDUARDO** looks from **EVA** to **ALFRED**.)*

It'll make me feel that I, like, know you, that we're close, that we're friends, it'll make me...happy.

(long pause)

*(**ALFRED** looks from **EVA** to **MELINDA**.)*

(Then he slowly acquiesces and nods.)

*(**EVA** crosses to **ALFRED** and kisses him gently on the cheek.)*

*(**EVA** is suddenly quite cheery:)*

EVA. *(cont.)* So: how did *you* two meet?

(pause)

Come on, you've heard all about our dirty laundry.

*(A strained laughter emits from **MELINDA**.)*

MELINDA. Eduardo's heard this a million times before.

EVA. I'm not Eduardo.

MELINDA. It's kinda boring.

EVA. I bet you a million bucks it's not.

EDUARDO. *(an attempt at levity)* It *is* kinda boring, actually.

EVA. I'll be the judge.

Come on. And feel free to embroider. Come on!

(pause)

MELINDA. Okay.

So.

We were in college.

(EVA pretends she's suddenly fallen asleep and starts snoring, a cartoon snore.)

(Everyone lets out some controlled polite laughter.)

MELINDA. I told you. It's boring.

EVA. Oh, I'm just kidding, you were in college, go on. Seriously. I'll behave.

MELINDA. And...

Well, my second semester...of Freshman year...I signed up for this human anatomy course.

(EVA does it again, nods off, snores. Little less laughter.)

(MELINDA is embarrassed.)

All right, I get the message, it's a cliché, we're such a cliché. I'm well aware.

EVA. No, I'm sorry, I couldn't resist, sorry, sorry, sorry.

I really do want to hear. I do. I promise not be to be a jerk. Please.

MELINDA. So: this anatomy class...You sure?

EVA. Yes, please.

ALFRED. Maybe we should...

EVA. I do. Please. I'm sorry. Go on.

MELINDA. Okay.

Well...Alfred was in the same class.

ALFRED. I was.

MELINDA. And we had this, like a group project, right? about the nervous system, or something...

ALFRED. Endocrine.

MELINDA. The endocrine system. And Alfred was in my group. And it was this big project that was due and one night we all decided, let's get together, let's have this giant study session in Alfred's dorm. And he came over to me, swaggered over actually (he'd had some beers)...and he leaned in to me...(Oh, I'll never forget this)...he leaned in and said...

(**EVA** *does it again.*)

(*This time she keels over on the couch, snoring very loudly, and she doesn't stop.*)

(*No one laughs.*)

(**MELINDA** *is visibly upset.*)

EDUARDO. Eva.
Eva!

MELINDA. It's okay. It's a silly story. Everyone knows how it ends. Obviously.

(*a beat, then —*)

(**ALFRED**'s *phone rings.*)

(*He looks at the number.*)

ALFRED. It's the sitter.

MELINDA. What?

ALFRED. I have to take this.

EDUARDO. Yeah, yeah.

MELINDA. What's wrong?

ALFRED. *(into cell)* Jennifer? Okay, calm down, it's normal, did you check the tube, the...check to see, there's a little valve...

(**MELINDA** *gestures for* **ALFRED** *to hand her the phone. He does.*)

MELINDA. Hi, Jen, it's me...everything okay? It happens all the time. No, I know. Hold on.

(She covers the handset.)

Do you think I should I go? I should go. You can stay.

ALFRED. She's fine. This is our one night. She has to learn this stuff.

MELINDA. I know, but...

ALFRED. Talk her through it. It's okay.

MELINDA. Jen, you still there? Hold on, you're breaking up. *(to* **EDUARDO,** *sotto voce)* Do you mind if?

*(***EDUARDO** *gestures "Yes, go!")*

*(***MELINDA** *goes off to the fire escape.)*

(pause)

*(***EVA** *suddenly sits up.)*

EVA. What I miss?

*(***EDUARDO** *gathers some of the dishes and heads off. He glares at* **EVA.***)*

EDUARDO. You wanna give me a hand?

EVA. I cook, you clean. Wasn't that the arrangement?

EDUARDO. I need to see you in the kitchen.

EVA. Alone in the kitchen?

EDUARDO. Eva!

EVA. Who are you again?

EDUARDO. Don't play games!

EVA. Yeah, sorry, my lover wouldn't want me meeting with strangers, alone, in the kitchen!

*(***EDUARDO** *starts off.)*

EDUARDO. *(under his breath) No puedo creer que, estés haciendo esto.* [I can't believe you're doing this.]

EVA. *(hissing back at him) Obtuviste, por lo que pagaste mi amor.* [You got what you paid for, lover!]

*(***EVA** *looks around the room.)*

Where's Belinda?

ALFRED. Melinda.

EVA. She sneaking a smoke?

ALFRED. Can I have my pants back?

EVA. What?

ALFRED. My pants.

EVA. Did something happen to your pants?

ALFRED. They should be dry by now. Can I have them back?

EVA. Your pants?

ALFRED. Yes.

EVA. Say please.

    (beat)

ALFRED. Is there something wrong with you?

EVA. I have sensitive teeth.

    My brother killed himself.

    My mother never loved me.

    Take your pick, pal.

ALFRED. Please! Just...

    Can I please have my pants back now, please?

EVA. Say pretty please.

    (beat)

ALFRED. Pretty please.

EVA. Beg me.

    (beat)

ALFRED. I beg you.

EVA. Beg me some more.

ALFRED. What?

EVA. You heard.

ALFRED. I...

EVA. You can do it.

ALFRED. I beg you some more.

EVA. Atta boy!

    *(**EVA** goes off.)*

(**ALFRED** *watches her go then quickly darts over to the draped statue and uncovers it. It's the most impressive of the series. There's something hugely disturbing about it, the twisted steel, the hideous body, but the face of the figure has this massive, placid, idiotic smile.* **ALFRED** *stares at it, then slowly reaches up to touch the face.*)

(*He hears* **EVA** *returning and quickly replaces the tarp over the statue. She enters and tosses* **ALFRED** *his pants.*)

EVA. *(cont.)* Put 'em on while they're still warm.

(*He struggles to get his pants on quickly.*)

Hey, did you notice?

Not once tonight did Eduardo refer to your wife by name.

ALFRED. Yes he did.

EVA. No. Don't think so. I told you, this is a point on which he's constantly confused. He doesn't know if her name's Melinda or Belinda. It's weird.

ALFRED. I've known Eduardo for fourteen years.

EVA. I know, right?

ALFRED. He's my oldest and dearest friend.

EVA. You're like brothers.

ALFRED. I'm sure you'll appreciate, at this point, if I take anything you say with a grain of salt.

EVA. Same here, Mr. Silver Lining, Mr. Brightside.

ALFRED. Okay. *(calling off)* Honey???

I don't know what I've done, if I've offended you in some way...

EVA. You're a total fake. You and your wife.

ALFRED. Honey!!!

EVA. Why do you think he invited you over here in the first place?

ALFRED. To meet you. He *likes* you. He's proud for his friends to...

EVA. Jesus, Alfie, weren't you paying attention?

Eduardo told me about you.

The happiest guy in the world.

Except he doesn't believe it.

(**ALFRED** *laughs.*)

He thinks you're full of shit.

And you haven't had the guts to ask him, because you know he's right.

ALFRED. We're leaving.

EVA. Ask him! Clean up some fucking dishes and go in the kitchen and ask him.

Why do you think he wanted you to meet me?

So we could become fast friends?

Have a polite little cocktail party?

It's my work, you lame-brain.

You're my homework.

For my project.

Look at your face: amazement!

Do you even know this guy? What have you two talked about for fourteen fuckin' years?

That's all he cares about. The work. Everything else is meaningless. Everything takes a back seat.

It's why *he's* distinguished himself in his field, and *you* have...withered into obscurity...no, no, not even obscurity because that presumes some *contribution* took place at some point...complacency...that's right, that's better. Complacency. Your so-called happiness has made you vanish. You're a creative eunuch.

Ask him.

Ask him.   .

Ask him.

For fuck sake. Just ask him.

(**ALFRED** *stares at* **EVA**.)

ALFRED. Eduardo!!!

(**EDUARDO** *enters from the kitchen.*)

EDUARDO. Everything okay?

(MELINDA comes in from the fire escape.)

MELINDA. Hey, guys, you want to know something funny?

(MELINDA laughs.)

While I was out there on the fire escape...while I was talking Jen down off the ledge, hearing Claire wheezing in the background...I looked down into the street and there is this SUV, middle of the block, sitting curbside, right there, right now. It's the guy, the same guy, the puddle guy, he looked up at me. He's sitting there, waiting for his next victim.

(EDUARDO grabs his coat and tears out the door.)

ALFRED. Eduardo.

Eduardo!!!

(ALFRED struggles to get his pants on and almost falls into the sculpture that's covered with a tarp. EVA has to steady it from toppling over.)

(We hear their footsteps going down the stairs.)

(EVA looks at MELINDA, lights a cigarette and stares at MELINDA.)

(MELINDA sits down on the couch. EVA pours her a glass of wine and she automatically starts sipping it.)

MELINDA. Claire sometimes has trouble breathing at night. The tubes get blocked.

There's this horrible rattling sound...it can really freak you out the first time you hear it.

Claire's fine.

Jennifer's new.

Everything's fine.

(blackout)

THREE

(Minutes later.)

*(**ALFRED** is hunched over on the couch. He is drenched from head to foot. His pant leg is ripped open at the knee and he is bleeding. Above his right eye he has another gruesome gash that is bleeding profusely. **EDUARDO** is trying to assist him but **ALFRED** is somewhat unco-operative, or disoriented, or both. **MELINDA** stands by helplessly with towels at the ready.)*

MELINDA. *(her usual mantra)* I close my eyes, I open my eyes. I close my eyes, I open my eyes.

ALFRED. That was a bad idea.

EDUARDO. Hold still, let me look.

> *(**EDUARDO** gingerly inspects **ALFRED**'s eye; **ALFRED** winces.)*
>
> Ayay!

MELINDA. What should I do? What should I do?

ALFRED. There's a joke, isn't there? 'What's the other guy look like?'

EDUARDO. I think you're gonna need stitches, brother.

ALFRED. I'll settle for a brandy.

> *(**EDUARDO** goes to the drinks table and makes **ALFRED** a brandy.)*
>
> Make it a double?

MELINDA. Does it hurt?

> *(**ALFRED** looks up at her through the blood, squinting.)*
>
> Dumb question, sorry.

(She crouches down before him. He sneers.)

ALFRED. How do I look? Tough? Streetwise?

MELINDA. It's starting to swell shut.

ALFRED. *(looking right at her)* You're slowly disappearing.

(He chuckles painfully.)

MELINDA. You're going to have a scar.

ALFRED. I've always wanted a scar.

MELINDA. Do you want a Tylenol?

ALFRED. I'd ask for some ice, but...*(calling off)* I know there's an embargo on that stuff 'round here.

(EDUARDO hands him the brandy and he downs it in a couple of big gulps. He hands the glass back.)

Yes please.

(EDUARDO goes to refill his glass.)

(EVA enters with a bag of frozen vegetables. She tosses them to ALFRED.)

EVA. Here ya go, bruiser!

ALFRED. California vegetable medley. Thank you, doctor.

EVA. What's the other guy look like?

(No one laughs, except ALFRED, who finds EVA's joke hysterically funny. He laughs until it hurts too much to laugh.)

MELINDA. What did you say?

ALFRED. Nothing.

MELINDA. Why did he hit you?

ALFRED. I have that kinda face?

MELINDA. Come on.

ALFRED. Boredom? Rage?

MELINDA. Alfred!

EVA. Mistaken identity?

EDUARDO. Eva.

ALFRED. Who knows. We crossed the street. He got out of his car. With his floppy hat. Eva was right. He was short. Like Napoleon.

EVA. *(as she exits)* Told you.

MELINDA. But *why?*

ALFRED. Napoleon was a complicated man.

(**EVA** *laughs at this, and starts out.*)

MELINDA. What did he hit you *with?*

ALFRED. His fist. I think. Eduardo?

EDUARDO. Rings on every knuckle.

EVA. *(from off)* Napoleon was a flashy dresser.

ALFRED. And then he threw me in the puddle. *(He inspects his knee.) His* puddle.

MELINDA. Well, you must have said something. People don't attack without provocation.

(**ALFRED** *laughs. It hurts to laugh.*)

ALFRED. Better tell Eva that. She seems to be exempt from that rule. Unless we're counting a pint of gin as provocation.

(**ALFRED** *laughs again. It hurts again.*)

EDUARDO. Hey, come on, man!

ALFRED. *(like it's a quote)* Speaking of gin...

(**ALFRED** *stands. He's a bit uncertain on his feet as his heads to the drinks table and pours a couple of fingers of gin into his glass.*)

MELINDA. Be careful.

ALFRED. I've never had an appreciation for gin until this very moment. *(looking through the glass)* I can see what she sees in this stuff. It gives you a kind of clarity. Hey, clear, Claire! That's what our daughter's name means.

MELINDA. Alfred, did *he* say anything to *you?*
This thug.

ALFRED. Which one?

MELINDA. The guy...the SUV!

ALFRED. I'm seeing two of everything, sorry.

MELINDA. When he hit you?

ALFRED. *I* didn't say anything. *He* didn't say anything.

EDUARDO. He didn't.

ALFRED. Eduardo said something.

Eduardo said, "You dumb piece of shit cocksucker,"... then something in Spanish I didn't quite catch. But given the diversity of the neighborhood, I'm assuming he understood both insults quite well.

(We hear **EVA***'s laughter from off.)*

Then, Eduardo, brute that he is, bent the guy's antenna.

And that's when Napoleon's three goons, equally short, all floppy-hatted, got out of the SUV and *that's* when we decided it was time to call it a night.

EDUARDO. I wanted to send a message.

ALFRED. A message?

*(***ALFRED*** smiles, but it looks more like a grimace.)*

What kind of pitiable message does bending a gang-banger's car antenna send?

EDUARDO. If you don't show guys like that you're willing to stand up to them they'll always take advantage.

*(***ALFRED*** snaps his finger at* **EDUARDO***.)*

ALFRED. You're right. Silver lining. This evening has taught me a valuable lesson: we have a responsibility to stand up to intimidation.

(he shouts off) Eva!

MELINDA. He could have had a gun.

You could have been killed.

It was stupid.

ALFRED. There she goes: blaming the victim.

MELINDA. I'm just saying, you shouldn't have gone down there in the first place, I don't know what you were thinking.

ALFRED. What *I* was thinking? I wasn't the aggressor. I barely had my pants back on if you recall. *I* was trying to thwart Eduardo's machismo, trying to prevent my *hombre* here from exercising some moronic brand of vigilante justice, that's what I was thinking. I don't know why you're yelling at me. Yell at him.

EDUARDO. Yell at me.

MELINDA. I'm not yelling at anyone. I feel sick. This has been a very strange night. *(She holds out her hands.)* Look at my hands, they're trembling. I want to go home.

ALFRED. No you don't.

MELINDA. Yes, I do.

ALFRED. We haven't had a night out in decades.

MELINDA. Stop exaggerating!

ALFRED. Stop yelling. Be happy. Be happy! Close your eyes, open your eyes, whatever you need to do to pull yourself together.

MELINDA. Jen keeps texting. You need stitches.

(ALFRED starts tearing off his wet clothing and tossing them to MELINDA.)

What are you doing?

ALFRED. Stripping away the layers.

MELINDA. We need to get you to the hospital, Alfred.

ALFRED. *(harshly)* I've spent the last fourteen years in hospitals!

MELINDA. *(re: his eye)* The bleeding's not going to stop by itself.

EDUARDO. She's right. You should go.

(ALFRED turns on EDUARDO.)

ALFRED. Is she? Is she right?

MELINDA. Yes, I am. Eduardo, can you call us a cab?

EDUARDO. No problem.

*(**EDUARDO** goes for the phone.)*

ALFRED. She has a name, you know.

EDUARDO. What?

ALFRED. She. My wife. Her. *(squints)* And her. Both of 'em.

EDUARDO. Are you okay, brother?

ALFRED. Am I okay? Of course I'm okay. I'm freakishly happy.
Isn't that right, *brother?*

MELINDA. Alfred, what's the matter with you?

ALFRED. Ask my brother.

MELINDA. What is he talking about?

ALFRED. Is it true, Eduardo, that you have some confusion surrounding my wife's name?

*(**EDUARDO** laughs.)*

EDUARDO. What?

MELINDA. He's clearly sustained a concussion.

ALFRED. No, no, I was having a little chat with Eva earlier, and she confessed to me...you think her name...is something other...than what her name actually is.

MELINDA. We've known Eduardo for years.

ALFRED. Fourteen years to be precise.
Which is why I initially disregarded Eva's assertion.
I've known Eduardo as long as I've known you. And I'm not tooting my own horn, but I've always known the name...sorry *names*...of the numerous women in Eduardo's life...even when, on occasion, I'd put good money on the fact he didn't have the foggiest what the *name(s)* of the numerous women he'd woken up beside *were*. So you see, brother, how it's not completely unfathomable. There's been more than one occasion you've called me in the wee hours and asked, 'Do you know who I went home with last night?' And I did, I always did, because that's what friends do, they pay attention.

MELINDA. Eduardo, I'm sorry...

EDUARDO. It's okay.

ALFRED. It's okay *what????* It's okay, Joan. It's okay, Barbara. It's okay, Genevieve.

EDUARDO. Jesus Christ!

MELINDA. He knows my name, Alfred. What's wrong with you?

ALFRED. Is it Melinda?
  Or Belinda?
  Melinda or Belinda?
  50/50 chance.
  Belinda or Melinda?
  Out of curiosity.

EDUARDO. You're drunk...

ALFRED. Yep, still...

EDUARDO. So I'm going to forgive you for being such a prick...
  And Eva...?

I love her, okay? And I know why she is the way she is.
  But *this*...this is embarrassing, for me, for your wife...

ALFRED. My wife...?

EDUARDO. Yes, your wife:

  (long pause)

  Melinda.

MELINDA. There.
  You should be ashamed. Eduardo, I am so...
  We're going.

  (ALFRED *is raging around the apartment like a madman.)*

ALFRED. No, we're not. We're not going home. We're happy people. We don't let minor aggravations get us down. Here's my pants.

  (He flings them at **MELINDA**.*)*

  I think better without them, it turns out. *(calling off)* Eva! I need to change!!! A robe, a towel, a blanket, a tarp??? *(to* **MELINDA***)* See if you can find a kimono or something for me to wear, I'm sure Eva has a kimono or something for me to wear. *(to* **EDUARDO***)* Something short and silky lying around the place, eh, Eduardo?

*(***ALFRED** *slaps his arm around* **EDUARDO***'s shoulders conspiratorially.)*

MELINDA. Alfred, you're mad!

ALFRED. No I'm happy! I'm so excrutiatingly happy! Everything in my life is exactly as I planned.

I never really wanted to be a writer.

I always wanted to teach French literature to disinterested students at a middling state college, and my dream has come true.

And for that, I am happy.

MELINDA. Sit down darling, please!

Eduardo, a cab.

EDUARDO. It's not a cab you need it's an ambulance. He's definitely got a concussion or something.

*(***EDUARDO** *goes to the phone and is about to dial 911 when* **ALFRED** *suddenly collides with the drinks table.* **EDUARDO** *goes to his assistance.)*

MELINDA. I think you've had enough.

ALFRED. I think I haven't.

*(***ALFRED** *pours some more wine into* **MELINDA***'s glass, but there's only a dribble left in the bottle.)*

Where's the hostess with the mostest? *(calling off)* Eva!!! More wine, *S'il te plaît* . Some of the good stuff. *(to* **EDUARDO***)* You don't mind do you? Eva said you've got an amazing stash back there. You've been holding out on us, brother.

EDUARDO. It's a few bottles.

ALFRED. Well, you better drink it up before Eva does. She's been dipping into it while you're at work. Oops, I wasn't supposed to say that. She resents the fact you're saving it for a rainy day, and frankly, so do I.

MELINDA. Honey.

ALFRED. What would you call this if not a rainy day? If the umpteenth birthdays and anniversaries we've shared together weren't occasion enough, what about this: after fending off your girlfriend all night, I've just gone head to head with Napoleon's army. *(calling off)* Eva!

EVA. *(off)* Is that my lover calling?

ALFRED. It's Alfred.

EVA. Who?

> *(Beat. He knows her game:)*

ALFRED. Alfie!

Your brother's lover, I mean your lover's brother. That's right, your brother didn't have a lover. That's why he killed himself.

> *(**ALFRED** laughs.)*

EDUARDO. Hey!!!

MELINDA. Alfred!!!

EDUARDO. Too much!!!

> *(**EVA** enters wearing a very short silk kimono.)*
>
> *(She is opening the bottle of wine in her hand.)*

ALFRED. Don't worry, darling, she shared that little intimacy with me when I arrived tonight.

Showing off her legs in her bath towel.

> *(**ALFRED** turns to **EVA**.)*

Is that my kimono?

EVA. I'm warming it up for you.

Want it?

ALFRED. Never mind, this'll do.

> *(**ALFRED** crosses to the one statue still draped in a tarp and tears it off. He wraps it around himself.)*

ALFRED. *(cont.)* Ah, finally we get to see your masterpiece.

(**ALFRED** *takes the bottle of wine from* **EVA**.)

Is this the good stuff?

EDUARDO. What are you doing?

EVA. Entertaining guests.

EDUARDO. Don't open that.

(**ALFRED** *pops the cork.*)

ALFRED. Is this the wine you bought with Elaine on your last foray, right before she split? It's no secret, brother, you sentimentally confessed to this secret stash on one of our first little mancations. You'd bought bottles and bottles, being so stupidly in love and then so stupidly bereft when Elaine up and left. The wine you vowed you'd never drink? Like some lugubrious character in a fucking French novel?

(**ALFRED** *laughs in* **EDUARDO***'s face.*)

EDUARDO. Enough, okay?

(**ALFRED** *takes a very long drink of the wine, much of it dribbles down his chin.* **EDUARDO** *reaches for the bottle, but* **ALFRED** *fends him off.*)

MELINDA. He doesn't do this, I'm sorry, he doesn't do this.

ALFRED. What was that dinky little town?

Something-*burg*, something-*ville*?

We ate heart-stopping steaks at this dive bar.

Decided to drink ourselves into oblivion.

To forget women. Then all we did all night was talk about them.

The girl, remember, the girl tending bar got off her shift and you charmed her, Eduardo, into joining us for drink after drink after drink and oh she was young and a little trashy and had a little space between her teeth, remember you mocked her, but she showed us how she could jet tequila across the bar and knock a playing card out of a shot glass.

And we laughed.

And then she told us about her tattoo.

And she was very cryptic.

About what it was, and *where* it was.

And I thought: I would give anything to see that tattoo. I would gladly quit my job, quit my life.

For just one glimpse.

MELINDA. Alfred, please!

ALFRED. And the next morning we went with our thick heads and our new Gal Friday to the county fair. And as we paraded through the center of town, with all these strangers who knew nothing of my life, my wife, my kid, I kept thinking, I could disappear, I could totally disappear, no one knows me here. I want to vanish into this crowd and never be seen or heard of again.

EVA. Like the kid in your story.

(**ALFRED** *stares at* **EVA.**)

The sleepwalker.

(*beat*)

ALFRED. It was the single happiest moment of my life.

And I looked across at you, brother, and you were whimpering again.

Over Elaine.

And I thought, fuck you, Eduardo! Fuck you!

You got your heart *bruised* like a teenage boy, you don't know what heartbreak is, try watching your own daughter dissolve into a flaccid little doll you have to cart about in a wheelchair and feed with a tube and slap diapers on and secretly hate.

And secretly hate.

(*Pause.* **MELINDA** *puts her face in her hands.*)

But wait, who am I referring to, it can't be me? I'm Alfred Rehm, I'm happy, I'm happy. And I'm supposed

to provide succor, for you, and you, and everyone
around me.

In spite of everything.

(**ALFRED** *goes upstage to* **EVA**'s *statue.*)

(*He takes up a piece of steel pipe and points to the head
of the statue.*)

Is that me or him?

EVA. Who?

ALFRED. Who!

Your fucking brother, that's who!

Who leapt to his death in the Winooski River.

(*He laughs loudly. And now, throughout, he ranges
around, circling* **EVA**, *scrutinizing her, the metal pipe
across his shoulder like a ballplayer.*)

While I was laying in that puddle out there, my eye
filling with blood, that's what went through my mind,
isn't that funny? Her brother's suicide. The way you
offered it. Like bait. Within minutes of my arrival. And
that's when it came to me. There was no suicide. There
likely was no brother. Eva's modus operandi. Saying
shit that may or may not be true just to provoke some
desired effect: the uncomfortability of others. Who
knows if anything she's said tonight is true. She's bril-
liant. She doesn't say anything you'd care to challenge
for fear of disrupting your own life or appearing cruel.
It's all done from a superbly defensible high ground.
She told me, for example, she lived with a guy who
hit her. Another little hand grenade. On the one hand
you feel sorry for her, on the other you're thinking:
one only needs to spend a little time with Eva to begin
to understand *why* he hit her.

(**MELINDA** *lets out an audible gasp.* **EDUARDO**
approaches **ALFRED**, *but he keeps him at bay with the
pipe.*)

EDUARDO. Jesus Christ, Alfred!

ALFRED. I know, I know what you're thinking: where's the Winooski River?

(He laughs; it really hurts.)

Which is *weirdly* the only thing I could think of as well to say after she dropped the whole brother's suicide bomb.

Eva is worse than the thug who cracked open my face tonight.

EDUARDO. You need to stop talking!

ALFRED. At least he's upfront about his antisocial behavior. This one's clever, this inscrutable little girl, this sphinx, (*to* **EDUARDO**) your enfant terrible with the sensitive teeth you brought home one drunk night. I admire her. It takes courage to be an utterly contemptible bitch!

EDUARDO. Get the fuck out of here!

ALFRED. An emotional terrorist posing as a sculptor.

*(**ALFRED** goes to the statue, swings the pipe and cleaves the head clear off the body. It drops to the floor with a terrible crash.)*

MELINDA. Oh, my god!!!

EDUARDO. Get him out of here.

*(**EDUARDO** dials 911. **ALFRED** crosses to **EVA**.)*

ALFRED. *(triumphant)* What do you think of that???

EVA. Thank you.

(beat)

ALFRED. What?

EVA. Thanks. For your honesty.
Finally.

ALFRED. I just destroyed your work, and you're thanking me?

EVA. It's not destroyed. It's finished.

*(**EVA** takes the bottle of wine back from **ALFRED**. She*

drinks.)

(EDUARDO crosses to ALFRED and hits him hard across the face.)

(ALFRED drops.)

EDUARDO. VERMONT.

(silence)

The Winooski River's in Vermont.

(ALFRED just stares up at EDUARDO.)

EDUARDO. I saw it when we went back home for her brother's funeral.
And the asshole who attacked you, is the asshole she lived with.

(EDUARDO snatches the bottle of wine back from EVA.)

(He grabs his coat and walks out.)

(ALFRED's cell phone chirps on the coffee table before MELINDA.)

(He's received a text.)

MELINDA. It's Jen.
She wants to know if we're ever coming home.

(ALFRED looks at MELINDA, then holds the bag of frozen vegetables to his face. MELINDA looks at EVA.)

Do you really think my hair would look better short?

(EVA nods.)

Give me the scissors.

(EVA hands them to her, sits beside ALFRED and lights a cigarette. ALFRED takes it from her and takes a long deep drag, blowing smoke into the air.)

ALFRED. Let me see your tattoo.

(MELINDA begins to snip off locks of her own hair as EVA turns to face ALFRED, very slowly opening her kimono to

reveal her tattoo as the lights begin to fade.)

MELINDA. I close my eyes, I open my eyes.

I close my eyes, I open my eyes.

(We hear the sound of an ambulance approach, which continues into the blackout.)

APPENDIX

I originally imagined that Alfred would be fairly short, and so wrote the sequence of lines that appears in the first confrontation scene with Eva. However, in subsequent productions the actors cast in the role of Alfred weren't really short. In fact, they were of average height, so I had to adjust the lines accordingly. I was never quite satisfied with the sequence of lines that accommodated taller Alfreds. I didn't think they were as funny as the lines I'd written originally, in which Eva makes fun of Alfred being short. And then it occurred to me that Eva is going to taunt Alfred regardless of how tall he is. Hence, the following alternate lines – which I think I like even more than the original ones. – RC

EVA. Hey, how tall are you?

ALFRED. *(The actor states his actual height.)* Err, five-ten.

EVA. Get out!

ALFRED. No, I'm...that tall.

EVA. You don't look that tall. You come across much shorter.

ALFRED. Okay.

EVA. Yeah, when Eduardo said, "My friend Alfred Rehm and his wife might be coming for dinner," I don't know I just pictured this guy who was, you know ... much taller.

*(**ALFRED** sets down his briefcase.)*

(He stands as erect as possible.)

ALFRED. Five ten's pretty tall.

EVA. But not tall, tall.
Is your wife tall?

ALFRED. Not really.

EVA. You sure about that?

ALFRED. Pretty sure.

EVA. She sounds tall.

ALFRED. She's not.

EVA. Sounds tall, tall.

Sounds taller than you.

ALFRED. I assure you she's not.

EVA. Well, she sounds it.

ALFRED. Based on…?

EVA. …Her name.

It's a tall name.

That's probably why!

ALFRED. Why what?

EVA. Musta pictured Belinda.

ALFRED. Melinda.

EVA: That's what I said.

Back to text.

SAMUEL FRENCH STAFF

Nate Collins
President

Ken Dingledine
Director of Operations,
Vice President

Bruce Lazarus
Executive Director,
General Counsel

Rita Maté
Director of Finance

ACCOUNTING

Lori Thimsen | Director of Licensing Compliance
Nehal Kumar | Senior Accounting Associate
Helena Mezzina | Royalty Administration
Glenn Halcomb | Royalty Administration
Jessica Zheng | Accounts Receivable
Andy Lian | Accounts Payable
Charlie Sou | Accounting Associate
Joann Mannello | Orders Administrator

CUSTOMER SERVICE AND LICENSING

Brad Lohrenz | Director of Licensing Development
Laura Lindson | Licensing Services Manager
Kim Rogers | Theatrical Specialist
Matthew Akers | Theatrical Specialist
Ashley Byrne | Theatrical Specialist
Jennifer Carter | Theatrical Specialist
Annette Storckman | Theatrical Specialist
Dyan Flores | Theatrical Specialist
Sarah Weber | Theatrical Specialist
Nicholas Dawson | Theatrical Specialist
Andrew Clarke | Theatrical Specialist
David Kimple | Theatrical Specialist

EDITORIAL

Amy Rose Marsh | Literary Manager
Ben Coleman | Editorial Associate
Caitlin Bartow | Assistant to the Executive Director

MARKETING

Abbie Van Nostrand | Director of Corporate
Communications
Ryan Pointer | Marketing Manager
Courtney Kochuba | Marketing Associate

PUBLICATIONS AND PRODUCT DEVELOPMENT

Joe Ferreira | Product Development Manager
David Geer | Publications Manager
Charlyn Brea | Publications Associate
Tyler Mullen | Publications Associate
Derek P. Hassler | Musical Products Coordinator
Zachary Orts | Musical Materials Coordinator

OPERATIONS

Casey McLain | Operations Supervisor
Elizabeth Minski | Office Coordinator, Reception
Coryn Carson | Office Coordinator, Reception

SAMUEL FRENCH BOOKSHOP (LOS ANGELES)

Joyce Mehess | Bookstore Manager
Cory DeLair | Bookstore Buyer
Jennifer Palumbo | Bookstore Order Dept. Manager
Sonya Wallace | Bookstore Associate
Tim Coultas | Bookstore Associate
Alfred Contreras | Shipping & Receiving

LONDON OFFICE

Felicity Barks | Rights & Contracts Associate
Steve Blacker | Bookshop Associate
David Bray | Customer Services Associate
Zena Choi | Professional Licensing Associate
Robert Cooke | Assistant Buyer
Stephanie Dawson | Amateur Licensing Associate
Simon Ellison | Retail Sales Manager
Jason Felix | Royalty Administration
Susan Griffiths | Amateur Licensing Associate
Robert Hamilton | Amateur Licensing Associate
Lucy Hume | Publications Manager
Nasir Khan | Management Accountant
Simon Magniti | Royalty Administration
Louise Mappley | Amateur Licensing Associate
James Nicolau | Despatch Associate
Martin Phillips | Librarian
Zubayed Rahman | Despatch Associate
Steve Sanderson | Royalty Administration Supervisor
Douglas Schatz | Acting Executive Director
Roger Sheppard | I.T. Manager
Panos Panayi | Company Accountant
Peter Smith | Amateur Licensing Associate
Garry Spratley | Customer Service Manager
David Webster | UK Operations Director

GET THE NAME OF YOUR CAST AND CREW IN PRINT WITH SPECIAL EDITIONS!

Special Editions are a unique, fun way to commemorate your production and RAISE MONEY.

The Samuel French Special Edition is a customized script personalized to *your* production. Your cast and crew list, photos from your production and special thanks will all appear in a Samuel French Acting Edition alongside the original text of the play.

These Special Editions are powerful fundraising tools that can be sold in your lobby or throughout your community in advance.

These books have autograph pages that make them perfect for year book memories, or gifts for relatives unable to attend the show. Family and friends will cherish this one of a kind souvenier.

Everyone will want a copy of these beautiful, personalized scripts!

ORDER YOUR COPIES TODAY!
E-MAIL SPECIALEDITIONS@SAMUELFRENCH.COM
OR CALL US AT 1-866-598-8449!